HEAVY ARTILLERY

I Was Junior Seau

GORDON KORMAN

HYPERION PAPERBACKS FOR CHILDREN
NEW YORK

Contents

HEAVY ARTILLERY

I Was Junior Seau

This Means War

The Monday Night Football Club couldn't do it alone. They needed an offensive line for the Arctic Iceman Cool Receiver Screen Pass. Nick Lighter, Coleman Galloway, and Elliot Rifkin regarded the three big bodies—six feet tall and rock solid from the ground up to their carrot noses.

Carrot noses?!

"Let me get this straight," Elliot said slowly. "We're using *snowmen* for the offensive line?"

"Pretty good, huh?" replied Nick, the quarterback. "I call them icemen because you never have to tell them to chill out. You guys will be linebackers. It's your job to break through the icemen and sack me."

"But I don't want my cold to get worse," Coleman protested.

"What cold?" scoffed Nick.

"Well, it's only a scratchy throat *now*," Coleman

admitted. "But it can turn into a sniffle, and then a postnasal drip. And before you know it, you're in the hospital with double pneumonia. At least, that's what happens when you wrestle a snowman the size of Junior Seau!"

But Elliot was hooked. "If we're on defense, who's the receiver? Who's going to catch the Arctic Iceman Cool Receiver Screen Pass?"

Nick pointed to another snowman on the side lawn just past the garage. "There he is. The coolest receiver in football."

Coleman squinted. "Why is he holding a bushel basket in his stick arms?"

"To make the catch," Nick explained. "If I get the ball in the basket, that counts as a completion. Come on, let's go."

The three best friends took their places. Even Coleman forgot his scratchy throat and crouched into a linebacker stance. Total effort was required for a trick play. It was the number two rule of the Monday Night Football Club. Only their weekly sleepovers to watch *Monday Night Football* were more important.

Nick crouched behind the snowman at center and barked, "Hut, hut, *hike!*"

Coleman and Elliot attacked the big icemen. Coleman pushed with all his might, but he could not budge his blocker. Elliot tried to sneak between two snowmen. Soon his parka was hopelessly entangled in the icemen's tree-branch arms.

Nick took aim at the cool receiver and reared back to throw.

Suddenly, a foghorn voice bellowed, *"You doofus! I'll pulverize you!"*

A blur in a bright blue ski jacket burst out the front door and sprinted toward the trick play.

Coleman and Elliot stared at the furious figure in full flight. "Hilary, Hilary, Heavy Artillery," they chorused.

Nick's eighth-grade sister barreled right over the center snowman, crushing it flat. She hit Nick just below the waist, clamping her arms around his hips. Before he could throw, Nick was driven hard into the snow of the front yard.

"What a sack!" breathed Elliot.

Nick gawked at her. "What was that for?"

"As if you didn't know!" Hilary growled down at him. "What rotten little low-down doofus took all my baby pictures out of the family album?"

"It wasn't me!" Nick defended himself.

"If those pictures aren't back by bedtime tonight, you're going to regret it for the rest of your very short life!" Hilary promised darkly. She jumped to her feet, executing a double karate kick that missed him by a hair. "Got it?"

Nick rose and brushed the snow from his parka. "Two martial arts classes, and you think you're Chuck Norris."

"Forget Chuck Norris," put in Elliot. "The way she busted through the line and sacked you—man, that looked like Junior Seau!"

"It's not a sack; it's a do-over," Nick insisted. "Hilary isn't part of the play."

"And I don't appreciate being compared to any of your Get-a-Life Club football muscleheads," Hilary added feelingly.

"But you yourself agreed what fantastic athletes they are," Coleman reminded her.

"Well, maybe the quarterbacks and the running backs have to be pretty good," she admitted. "But not the guys on defense. How much talent does it take to be big as a planet and meaner than a sewer rat?"

"I can't believe what I'm hearing!" cried Nick. "A defensive star like Junior Seau is like a miracle! He defies the laws of nature! To be *that* big and *that* strong, but also *that* fast—"

"Fast?" she snorted. "Who needs speed? The ball-carrier comes to you, and you tackle him. Big deal."

"That's it!" roared Nick. "Get out of here! Anybody who knows that little about football has no right to be on the same field as the Arctic Iceman Cool Receiver Screen Pass!"

"Don't think you can change the subject on me, doo-fus," Hilary seethed. "Those pictures had better be back where they belong tonight." And she stormed away, practicing karate chops as she walked. She stomped into the house and slammed the door.

Elliot thrust out an imaginary microphone for the postgame interview. "Tell the folks at home, Nick. How does it feel to be sacked over baby pictures?"

"I only swiped them for *her*," Nick defended himself. "Sunday is Hilary's birthday, and her crazy friends are planning a surprise party."

"And now a word from our sponsor," Elliot prompted.

"How about a public service announcement?" Nick suggested. "Board up your windows, sandbag your homes. Hilary is having another wild party."

"I can't believe your parents gave permission," commented Coleman.

"Who said anything about permission?" asked Nick. "My folks will be in Boston all day. And we'll be over at Elliot's watching the Pro Bowl. Hilary can trash the whole house for all I care."

"So why do they need baby pictures?" asked Elliot.

"Her friend Katrina has one of those giant fake cakes," Nick explained. "You know, the plywood kind that people can jump out of? They're going to use it for Hilary's party, so they want to decorate it with old snapshots."

"Who's going to jump out?" Coleman wanted to know.

Nick grinned. "Seth Kroppman."

"I thought he and Hilary broke up," put in Elliot.

"Those two knuckleheads break up and get back together again every five minutes. They're in love, but they're always fighting. Who knows?" He made a face. "If I'm that stupid when I get to eighth grade, promise you'll shoot me."

"We won't be like that," Coleman vowed. "We've got Monday Night Football Club to keep us from going crazy."

"Not to mention the Eskimos sweater," added Elliot. "Who could worry about anything else when we've got *that*?"

The sweater had been left to Nick by his late grandfather, who had played college football for the North Brainerd Eskimos. It was ugly and hot and itchy, but it had one extremely special quality. Anyone who fell asleep wearing it would somehow be transported into the body of a famous football star. It had allowed the Monday Night Football Club members to play in big games, and even the Super Bowl!

"Speaking of the sweater," Coleman said to Nick, "have you decided if you're going to try it out during the Pro Bowl?"

"I'm in," Nick replied fervently. "I mean, nothing is as important as the Super Bowl. But this game is different. In the Pro Bowl, every single player on the field is an amazing all-star. Every pass, every run, every tackle, every kick is coming from one of the best in the NFL. How can you miss a chance to be a part of it?"

At that moment, Nick's bedroom window opened, and an avalanche of football pennants and T-shirts tumbled out into the slushy bushes.

"Nick! Your stuff!" cried Coleman.

"Wow," commented Elliot. "Hilary, Hilary, Heavy Artillery's going to feel pretty guilty when she finds out you only stole those pictures for *her* party."

"She'll owe me big," Nick smirked as the last few items buried themselves softly in the snow.

Coleman pointed. "Hey, isn't that the poster of Junior Seau from your wall?"

"What?" And Nick was off, yelling, *"Hil-a-ry!!"*

Hilary thumbed her nose out the window. "Got you last!"

Coleman joined Elliot, who was already rebuilding the flattened snowlineman for the Arctic Iceman Cool Receiver Screen Pass. "You know what this means?" he asked, lending a hand.

Elliot nodded. "War."

Sploosh!

Hilary Lighter paused in the doorway of Nick's bedroom. Down the hall she could hear the theme music of the *Sport Report*. She was safe. Her brother wouldn't notice a tidal wave when there was something about football on TV. Nobody on earth was as football crazy as the founder of the Monday Night Football Club. He even had the initials N. F. L. for Nicholas Farrel Lighter.

Nick's posters covered every inch of the room like wallpaper. A fierce player with a lightning bolt on his helmet and a body like a gladiator caught her attention. JUNIOR SEAU read the caption under the fearsome photograph.

"If he's Junior," Hilary mumbled to herself, then I'd hate to run into Senior!"

Junior was a little soggy from the snow, but every single poster and pennant was back in place. And Hilary's baby pictures were still missing. It wasn't fair! She needed to think of some way to get back at Nick.

Then he'd *have* to return those old photos.

She snapped her fingers. The shirt.

Why Nick and his Get-a-Life Club buddies loved that ratty old rag Hilary would never understand. It was itchy, ancient, not to mention ugly—chocolate brown with the orange number thirteen.

Yet they treated that moth-eaten sweater like it was worth a million dollars. One of them always seemed to be wearing it when the guys got together to watch *Monday Night Football*.

Through careful spying, Hilary had discovered the supersecret hiding place where Nick kept the jersey. She slipped into Nick's room and rummaged in the closet. She unwrapped a San Diego Chargers blanket to reveal an old typewriter case. The locks snapped open, and out spilled the Eskimos shirt.

Running her fingers over the scratchy wool, she felt a pang of guilt. Their grandfather had left this to Nick, not her.

But Grandpa was part of a different generation, she told herself. In the old days, you'd never give an athletic uniform to a girl!

That wasn't true anymore—especially not for Hilary, who was captain of every girls' sports team at Middletown Junior High. So, in a nineties way, she was almost *co-owner* of this football shirt. Because a modern Grandpa would have left it to both of them.

She nodded positively. This wasn't stealing. She was just taking what was rightfully hers. Well, half hers.

She closed up the supersecret hiding place so Nick wouldn't suspect anything. Then she smuggled the sweater into her own room and stuffed it under her pillow.

She joined her family in the TV room, beaming her best sisterly smile. "Anything good on the *Sport Report*?"

Nick matched her grin. "The Pro Bowl is tomorrow, so the broadcast is live from Hawaii. The NFL is having a big luau for the players tonight."

"Now, that's more like it," approved Mrs. Lighter. "You two should be best friends instead of bickering all the time."

"Right, Mom," they chorused.

But brother and sister concealed exactly the same thought: he's/she's up to something.

Nick crept down the darkened hallway to his sister's bedroom. He put his ear to the closed door. He could hear the sounds of thrashing and sheet tossing.

Yep, she was asleep, all right. Hilary slept like a Mixmaster. Every morning she arose from such a tangle of blankets and pillows that it looked like a hurricane had passed through the room.

He dropped to his hands and knees and felt around the thick carpet. He found the string and grabbed it. The other end was tied around the fat water balloon that Nick had placed on the bookshelf above his sister's bed. She always took so long in the bathroom that there had been plenty of time for him to run the string behind the bed and along the baseboard to the door.

In the darkness, Nick grinned. Revenge was going to be sweet. Hilary would rue the day that she had thrown his football stuff out into the snow!

Hilary had been asleep for less than an hour, and already the covers were kicked onto the floor, and her pillow was across the room. Her face was buried in the Eskimos sweater. She was even more restless than usual because of the scratchy wool on her skin.

Little did Hilary know that sleep was what triggered the mysterious power of the Monday Night Football Club's treasured shirt. As she slept, a tiny glowing football—just about the size of a lima bean—appeared over her head. It danced in the air, tracing out the number *55*. Then it winked out like a disappearing firefly.

Hilary looked around in the dim glow of the bonfire.
Bonfire?!
A soft breeze rustled through the palm trees—*palm trees?!* The beach was crowded, and girls in grass skirts were dancing the hula—*hula?!*—while the waiters displayed a giant roast pig on a platter.
Oh, Hilary thought contentedly. *A vacation in Hawaii. What a great dream to have in the dead of winter.* She lay back in the sand and smoothed the fabric of her glow-in-the-dark flowered shirt. . . .

Nick tugged on the string, and the water balloon toppled off the shelf.

Sploosh!

It exploded right on Hilary's head.

Her scream was most satisfying. "Got you last," Nick whispered to himself.

He dropped the string and bounded back to his own bed. It was his plan to be innocently snoring by the time Hilary figured out what had hit her.

The stampede in the hall meant that Mom and Dad had heard the scream, too.

"Honey, honey, are you okay?" panted Mr. Lighter.

"The doofus water-bombed me!"

"That's impossible!" exclaimed Mrs. Lighter. "He's fast asleep!"

A wild-eyed Hilary appeared at the door, her wet hair straggling around her ears. She held up a broken balloon at the end of a long string. "Then what's this— an underwater kite?"

Nick blew his cover. He laughed.

The next ten minutes were filled with screaming accusations from the two younger Lighters.

"You threw my football stuff in the snow!"

"That doesn't give you the right to drown me!"

"You messed up my trick play!"

"Because you stole my baby pictures!"

"Did not!"

"Did so!"

"E-nough!!" Mr. Lighter's voice echoed through the house. "I don't want to hear another word out of either of you! You are brother and sister!"

Hilary made a face. "I *was* an only child until *he* came along!"

Nick glared at her. "Well, if I'd known *you* were here, I'd have gone someplace else!"

Mr. Lighter gestured helplessly towards his wife. "They're crazy!"

"The fighting in this family is at an end," Mrs. Lighter stated firmly.

"But that's no fair!" Hilary blurted. "He got me last!"

"Tough," said Nick.

"Yes, it is," their mother nodded. "But not nearly as tough as it will be on both of you if I catch you fighting again."

Mr. and Mrs. Lighter slammed back into their own room.

Nick couldn't resist sending a self-satisfied smirk in his sister's direction.

She responded with her trademark move, the double karate kick. The wind from it nearly knocked him over.

A Sweater to Sweat in

"Honey, are you sure you're not upset?" asked Mr. Lighter, knotting his tie. "I hate to leave you on your birthday."

"Don't worry, Dad," smiled Hilary. "Business is business. You guys can't let Mr. Nakamura have dinner alone on his last night in America."

Her mother stepped into her high heels. "I still wish my company didn't need me to go to Boston today of all days. We could have had such a lovely family evening together."

Hilary snorted. "On the night of the Pro Bowl game? I know one member of this family who wouldn't think it was so lovely."

Mrs. Lighter shrugged into her coat. "Well, then Nicky would have learned a lesson about family loyalty."

Mr. Lighter laughed out loud. "I think the family would have learned a lesson about *Nicky's* loyalty to football." He turned to his daughter. "Thanks for being such a good sport, honey. We promise you a first-class birthday dinner tomorrow."

"You're on, Dad."

The Lighters gave a happy-birthday honk on the horn as they started on the ninety-minute drive to Boston. Hilary waved them out of sight and wandered back into the house.

Nick, Coleman, and Elliot were glued to the TV screen watching the all-day festivities that led up to the Pro Bowl.

"Happy birthday, Hilary," said Coleman.

"Yeah, happy birthday," echoed Elliot.

"Thanks guys," Hilary said. "I appreciate it. Especially since I didn't get so much as a 'Go jump in the lake' from my loving brother."

Nick looked at her impatiently. "Don't you have karate class?"

In a few minutes." She stared at the TV in sudden shock. "What's that?"

"It's the Pro Bowl luau from last night," Elliot explained. "Look, there's Junior Seau, eating up a storm."

Hilary gawked. The big football star was wearing a very familiar glow-in-the-dark flowered shirt.

Where had she seen that before? Then she remembered. Her dream last night. She frowned. It seemed like the whole thing was on TV: bonfire, hula dancers, roast pig!

How could she dream about a party she didn't even know existed? And what was that Junior Seau guy doing in her shirt?

"Are you okay?" Coleman asked in concern. "You look like you've seen a ghost."

"I—I'm okay." Hilary shook off her confusion. Maybe she was just remembering wrong.

Old age, she thought. She was fourteen today.

Besides, she'd only dreamed the luau for a second. Then a nasty, low-down skunk had dropped a water balloon on her. Anybody could have messed up the details.

She watched Junior Seau and some of the other players joining the hula dancers. The party looked so familiar. . . .

She turned to Nick. "Make sure you lock up when you go to Elliot's for Get-a-Life Club."

"That's Monday Night Football Club!" Nick roared back in outrage.

"Today is Sunday," Hilary teased, "or haven't you noticed?"

Nick sprang to his feet. "The Super Bowl and the Pro Bowl both count as official Monday nights!" he snapped. "So even though it's Sunday, it's Monday! It's the last football for six whole months, and I refuse to let you wreck it for me! Now go practice your karate kicks!"

As she left the TV room, Hilary heard Elliot whisper, "Don't forget to bring the sweater to my place."

"Are you kidding?" Nick hissed back. "I'd forget my own head before I'd forget the sweater."

She smiled secretly. The doofus wasn't going to have his precious sweater because he wasn't going to be able to find it. She packed up her duffel for karate class. Then she pulled the Eskimos shirt from its hiding place under her pillow, and stuffed it into the bag with her white *gi*.

Got you last, she thought with a grin.

She hesitated. Mom had promised big trouble if there was any more fighting. This probably counted as fighting.

But she wasn't stealing it *now*, she reminded herself. She stole it yesterday, long before the no-fighting rule came down. So this was okay.

"Enjoy the Pro Bowl," she called in her sweetest tone. She couldn't stop grinning for the entire walk to the community center.

Martial arts class didn't start on time. The community center's furnace was broken, and the karate dojo was fifty degrees.

Hilary huddled on a folding chair, hugging herself and shivering. The other girls were a hilarious sight, with their bare feet wrapped in scarves and heavy coats.

The teacher tried to put a good face on things. "Don't worry," he assured everyone. "The engineer is working in the boiler room this very minute. Meanwhile, if you've got a sweater, I suggest you put it on and do some stretches."

Yeah, sure, thought Hilary. Who brings a sweater to sweat in?

Then she remembered. She *did* have something warm—the Eskimos shirt. She smiled to herself. Wouldn't Nick have a fit if he knew she was actually wearing it?

She went into the locker room, plucked the brown jersey out of the duffel, and pulled it down over her head.

"Holy moly!" she exclaimed aloud. "This thing must be woven out of itching powder!"

It was unbearable—hot and scratchy and heavy and hideous. She couldn't believe Nick actually *liked* this torture device. Heck, she couldn't believe Grandpa hadn't thrown it in the garbage instead of passing it down like a family heirloom. The old man had saved it for fifty years so he could leave it to his grandson. *Why?*

She put her hand to her brow. She was sweating! Nobody could perspire in an ice-cold locker room. Grandpa's football jersey was a portable furnace!

Hilary yawned hugely. The sheer heat and weight of this awful thing was making her drowsy.

And it didn't help that she'd been woken up in the middle of the night by a water balloon! She was really tired.

She lay back on the bench. Her eyes closed.

She shook herself. They'd fix the furnace, and she'd end up snoozing through karate class!

But she couldn't bring herself to get up. She felt like she was in a sauna. Her eyelids weighed twenty pounds each. She didn't have the strength to keep them open— not when she was relaxing, nodding, drowsing. . . .

As Hilary drifted into sleep, the small glowing football appeared above her nose. Once again, it traced out two fives and disappeared.

This Isn't Me

The roar of the water was all around Hilary as she balanced on the surfboard. She glanced to the rear. The giant wave curled over her shoulder like a huge mouth about to swallow her whole.

Instant terror. *I don't know how to surf!*

And then she was on her way, skimming the ocean at breathtaking speed. The wind whistled in her ears. She slalomed like an expert towards the shore.

It's the dream again! I'm back in Hawaii!

She crouched down on the board and held out her arms. She was determined to enjoy this while it lasted. When the big wave wiped her out, for sure she was going to wake up in the locker room at karate class in the middle of a freezing cold winter.

The breaker hit the shore like a ton of bricks. Hilary was tossed every which way in the warm turquoise water. And when she sat up, exhilarated, in the surf—

I'm still here!

This must have been some newfangled industrial-strength dream. It felt totally real, everything was in living color, and it was impossible to wake up.

I know. I'll pinch myself.

The hand that reached out was massive. The forearm it was about to pinch was as thick as an oak tree.

"*This isn't me!*" she cried out. The voice was low and rumbling.

In horror, Hilary clamped both hands over her mouth.

That's a guy's voice! Not just a guy; a grown man!

Terrified, she ran up the beach. Maybe she could check her reflection in the glass wall of the hotel.

I can't see myself! she thought in frustration. *If only that great big barrel-chested weight lifter would get out of the way . . .*

Nervously, she clutched at her hair. The great big barrel-chested weight lifter reflected in the glass did the same.

"He's me!" she blurted in that deep voice. "I mean, I'm him! I mean—I don't know what I mean!"

Had she gone crazy? What was going on here? Two minutes ago she was in the community center waiting for someone to fix the furnace. Now she was in Hawaii—and that was the most believable part of all this! She was a guy! A man! A big one! She—the guy—even looked kind of familiar.

"Hey, Junior," called a voice behind her.

She wheeled. "Just who are you calling Junior—"

She froze. Everybody knew that face. It was on the biggest billboard in Middletown—the one advertising the *Sport Report*. It was John Elway, the legendary quarterback of the Denver Broncos.

Elway laughed. "It's your name, isn't it?"

Of course! Hilary wheeled to stare at herself in the glass. The last time she'd seen that face it was sticking out of a glow-in-the-dark shirt at a luau on TV! It was Junior Seau!

She—Hilary Lighter—was Junior Seau! But how?

"Come on," Elway urged. "The bus picks us up in half an hour."

"Bus?" Hilary repeated. "Are we going somewhere?"

Elway frowned. "Did that surfboard come down on your head? We got picked for the Pro Bowl. It might be nice if we showed up for the game."

Hilary pinched herself again, hard this time. It wasn't a dream. But it *couldn't* be real!

Could it?

"Hilary, wake up! The heat's back on!"

Junior Seau opened his eyes. A young girl stood over him, shaking him by the shoulder. She was wearing strange white pajamas.

"What are you doing here?" he challenged her. "Who let a girl into the locker room?"

"It's the *girls'* locker room," she laughed. "Come on. Class is starting."

"Class?" Seau sat up. "What class? Where's John?"

What was wrong with his voice? He must have been dead asleep to wake up all squeaky like that.

The karate student frowned. "John? John who?"

"John Elway!"

She goggled. "John Elway the *football* player?"

"We were on the beach together," Seau told her.

The girl snorted. "You have great dreams, Hilary. Now hurry up. Everybody's waiting." And she left the room.

Hilary? Who was Hilary?

Seau stood up, head spinning. As soon as he was on his feet, he knew something wasn't right. The floor was too close to his head. His whole body felt light, like it was filled with air. Strands of long hair were tickling his ears. Boy, did he need a haircut—

Whoa!!

His image in the mirror made him jump back. He wasn't himself any more! He was a *girl*! He flexed a puny arm. What happened to his muscles? His face? His *life*?

"I can't be a girl!" he blurted. "I'm a married man!"

It came out the wailing of a teenybopper.

Breathing hard in his panic, he staggered out of the locker room. He stopped short. A dozen young girls stood watching him. All were wearing those funny pajamas—now he could see they were martial arts uniforms. He was wearing one, too, under this itchy jersey.

"Welcome, Hilary," the instructor greeted him. "Why don't you get rid of that heavy sweater, and we can start right in with the warm-up."

Bewildered, Seau pulled off the brown shirt and

tossed it in a corner. Shouldn't he be doing something about this? Like screaming the place down, demanding to know what had happened to him? Was he the only one who'd been kidnapped away from his own body?

"Psssst!" he whispered. "Are any of the rest of you girls like me? You know—a professional football player?"

It got a huge laugh.

"Come on!" Seau persisted. "Be serious! Who else is here for the Pro Bowl?"

The girl next to him looked puzzled. "Here in karate class?"

"No! Here in Honolulu!"

Wordlessly, she pointed out the picture window. Four inches of snow blanketed the parking lot.

Junior Seau stared. In Hawaii?

How Come There's Popcorn
All over the Floor?

Hilary's friends swarmed all over the living room like ants. A big banner that read

HILARY
YOU'RE THE GREATEST FRIEND!
HAPPY BIRTHDAY

was draped across the far wall. From it, hundreds of pink and silver streamers dangled like the legs of a caterpillar. Bowls of chips, popcorn, and pretzels were balanced on every shelf and tabletop. The rug was rolled up and standing in the corner, leaning against a styrofoam cooler loaded with ice and soft drinks. A six-foot tower of CDs stood in readiness beside the stereo.

Katrina Winslow, Hilary's best friend and organizer of the party, was blowing up balloons from a helium tank. More than half were overinflating and exploding.

"I hope you brought a thousand balloons," Nick commented, "because you've already busted nine hundred."

Pow!

"Nine hundred and one," Nick corrected.

She glared at him. "Remember, you promised to leave before the party starts."

"First I want to see the cake," said Nick. "The one Seth's going to jump out of. Where is it?"

"Oh, it's not here yet," Katrina replied. "It's just girls at first. The guys aren't coming over until later. They'll bring Seth and the cake."

"That dumb cake almost got me killed," Nick put in sourly. "Hilary's on the warpath over those baby pictures you made me steal for it."

"Don't worry," soothed Katrina. "Tonight she'll see them on the cake, and you guys will be friends again."

"Yeah," Nick snorted sarcastically. "And the moon will fall out of the sky and get stuck on the Statue of Liberty's torch."

The doorbell rang.

Katrina was horrified. "Oh no! Hilary's early! Quick everybody—*hide*!"

Nick watched in high amusement as seventeen eighth-graders scrambled under tables, around corners, behind furniture, and into closets. Katrina knocked over three bowls of snacks in her crazed effort to get the helium tank out of sight.

Nick opened the door to admit Coleman and Elliot.

"Getting close to game time," Coleman said cheerfully. "Hey, how come there's popcorn all over the floor?"

Hilary's friends began to appear from their hiding places.

Katrina was annoyed. "You said you'd be gone."

"And we're going," Nick promised. "We just have to get one thing first."

The Monday Night Football Club sauntered down the hall, crunching spilled potato chips under their feet.

"Boy, your mom is going to freak out when she sees her house," Elliot murmured. "And the party hasn't even started yet."

Nick ushered them into his room and shut the door. "That's why I want to be safe and sound in your basement when Mom and Dad come home and find thirty eighth-graders smashing the place into toothpicks. Believe me, the NFL did me a big favor when they planned the Pro Bowl for Hilary's birthday."

"Let's get the shirt and get out of here," urged Coleman uneasily. "Hilary's friends are dangerous."

Through the door they could hear the high-pitched munchkin voices of the girls talking with mouthfuls of helium.

The three fell silent as Nick reached into the back of his closet and pulled out the Chargers blanket. He unwrapped it carefully to reveal the typewriter case. Nick snapped open the locks and lifted the lid.

His mouth fell open, and all the blood in his veins turned to ice. The gasp that came from him was barely human.

"It's gone!" squeaked Coleman.

Helpless with shock, Nick overturned the typewriter case and shook it, hoping against hope that the brown sweater would magically reappear. A small square of paper fell out and fluttered to the floor.

Nick pounced on it. He read aloud: "You'll get your precious shirt back when my baby pictures have been returned to the family album—Hilary."

"Hilary, Hilary, Heavy Artillery!" chorused Coleman and Elliot in agony.

"But how could she know about the supersecret hiding place?" Coleman wailed.

"Well, obviously it's not as supersecret as we thought," snarled Nick.

"You—you don't think she'd *wear* it, do you? You know—try to switch with somebody?"

"Impossible," said Nick. "Nobody knows about that except the three of us."

Elliot sighed. "This stinks, Nick. There goes your chance to play in the Pro Bowl. But at least we know the sweater is safe and we're going to get it back eventually."

"We're going to get it back *now*!" growled Nick. "Even if we have to take Hilary's room apart molecule by molecule!"

The Monday Night Football Club marched into the next bedroom and began a search worthy of the FBI. They emptied the closet, examined every drawer, and pulled the mattress and box spring off the bed. They rifled through the laundry hamper, checked behind the bookcase, even felt under the carpet. Nothing.

Nick snapped his fingers. "I'll bet she has it with her."

"What for?" asked Coleman.

Elliot supplied the answer. "To keep it away from us."

"So all we have to do," Nick decided, "is wait for her to come home."

Coleman was horrified. "What are we going to do— wrestle her for her sports bag? Hilary, Hilary, Heavy Artillery is a lethal weapon! And now she knows all that karate stuff!"

Elliot rolled his eyes. "A week ago, you were Mr. Fearless in the Super Bowl," he told Coleman. "And now you're scared of Nick's sister."

"Aren't you forgetting something?" Coleman scowled. "I was Mr. Fearless because I was *Dan Marino*! Today I'm just plain me."

"You mean Mr. Gutless?" asked Elliott.

"Mr. *Careful*," Coleman corrected.

"It doesn't matter," Nick interrupted.

"Hilary won't even notice what happens to her bag. She'll be the guest of honor at a surprise party. Trust me—it can't miss."

Katrina stuck her head in the door. "Why are you guys still here? Karate class is over in five minutes. Hilary will be home soon!"

"There's been a change of plan," Nick replied. "We need to hang around for the beginning of the party. But don't worry. We won't get in the way."

Katrina whistled, and a dozen girls appeared. The three members of the Monday Night Football Club were bundled into their winter coats and thrown out into the snow. Nick barely had a chance to grab his sleeping bag from the front hall before Katrina slammed the door and locked it.

Nick shook his fist at the house. "I live here, you know!"

"She doesn't care," Coleman said sadly. "Eighth-graders don't care about anything."

Dear Mr. Seau

SEAU, JUNIOR. SEX: M. HEIGHT: 6'3". WEIGHT: 250 LBS.

Hilary examined the driver's license in the dark. The blinds were tightly drawn in Junior Seau's hotel room.

Unbelievable! She glanced at the mirror above the dresser. *That's my face! I'm Junior Seau! And I'm not still asleep in the locker room at karate class! All this is real.*

Somewhere there had to be a clue to what was happening. She flipped through the superstar's wallet. What did she expect to find? A letter from Publishers Clearing House saying, "Congratulations! Ed McMahon has picked your name, and you are the new Junior Seau?"

Don't get cute, Hilary! You're in big trouble here! Concentrate!

Social Security ID, wedding picture—*hmmm, pretty wife*—credit cards, a claim check for dry cleaning. She turned her attention to the suitcase. There it was—the glow-in-the-dark shirt! She held it up. Hilary and at least half her friends could have fit in there!

She ignored the clothes and dug deeper. There was a shoehorn, a golf ball, and—what was this? She pulled out a bundle of letters, slipped off the elastic band, and began to sort through them. She scanned the postmarks: New York, California, Kansas, Alaska, New Mexico . . .

These were fan letters! Wow! Junior Seau was even more famous than she'd realized! And a pretty nice guy, too—he read all his mail, even when he had important things like the Pro Bowl on his mind.

Hilary shook her head in admiration. Some of these letters were from places as far away as Canada, England, and Japan. Hey, here was one from Middletown!

She stared. That was *her* home address. This was a letter from *Nick*! She held it up to the light and squinted to see if she could read what the doofus had written. She made out "Dear Mr. Seau," and then a knock at the door startled her. The letter dropped from her hand and slipped under the sofa.

She got down on her hands and knees and felt around for it. But her big fingers touched only carpet.

"Junior?" It was John Elway. He knocked again.

Without thinking, Hilary reached out a massive paw and lifted the sofa like it weighed nothing. She froze.

This thing must be a hundred and fifty pounds! Look at me — I'm Hercules!

"Junior, are you in there or what? The bus leaves in five minutes!" Elway was beginning to sound annoyed.

Hilary retrieved the letter and set the sofa back in place. "I'll meet you in the lobby," she called in Junior

Seau's voice. With a half-smile, she reached for a piece of hotel stationery and a pen. "I have to write a quick letter."

Smack!

The karate kick caught Junior Seau full in the face. He staggered back, stunned.

"Come on, Hilary," encouraged the instructor. "You've got to be more aggressive. You've got to fight back."

Seau looked at his opponent. She was five foot nothing and weighed maybe ninety pounds. Junior Seau could never hit a girl—even though, for some crazy reason, he was a girl, too!

Thud!

Her small tight fist came up and belted him.

"Ow!"

Why did this hurt so much? In the NFL, he took hits that would derail a train. If he had his *real* body, he wouldn't feel this any more than a mosquito bite. But as Hilary, he was getting clobbered. And he couldn't fight back!

Whack!

Now his nose was bleeding.

The teacher blew his whistle. "All right, that's enough for today. Here, Hilary, use my towel."

One by one, the girls shrugged into their coats and left the community center. Seau sat on a folding chair, his head thrown back, nursing his nosebleed. He was half hoping that his nose would bleed forever. He certainly had no idea where he was supposed to go from here—or where this Hilary person lived.

Should he contact the police? He struggled with the details of his story: "I know I look like a junior high cheerleader, but I'm actually the most feared linebacker in the AFC." Oh, that would be a hit. They'd lock him up and throw away the key.

He removed the red-spotted towel. The karate teacher was watching him anxiously.

"You're not yourself today, Hilary."

"You'll never know how right you are," said Junior Seau nasally.

The man smiled. "Get your stuff together. I'll drop you off at home."

Seau sighed with relief. At least he had a place to lie low and see what he could do to get back to his own life. Maybe all he needed was peace and quiet—a chance to think this out.

Seau opened the front door of the Lighter house with the key from Hilary's coat pocket. He stepped into the darkened front hall.

Suddenly, the lights blazed on, and seventeen girls leaped up out of nowhere, hurling confetti in his face.

"Surprise!!"

Seau jumped back as if he'd been burned, dropping the duffel bag at his feet. He took in his surroundings: streamers, balloons, and a big pile of brightly wrapped presents. The girls began to sing "Happy Birthday."

"Are you surprised?" crowed Katrina.

"Blown away," admitted Seau.

Just beyond the porch, a bush moved. Three heads appeared. Six eyes fixed themselves on Hilary's gym bag.

"There it is, right by the door," whispered Elliot.

As the partying girls led the guest of honor into the living room, the Monday Night Football Club approached the house. Nick snatched up the bag, unzipped it, and dumped the contents out on the front stoop. The first item to hit the snow was the Eskimos jersey.

Nick hugged it close to his heart. "Oh man, I was worried about you, buddy!"

Coleman reached out and brushed the sleeve. "Itchy as ever," he said admiringly.

"Perfect timing," agreed Elliot. "Let's get over to my place. The Pro Bowl pregame starts in two minutes."

They ran.

A Busload of Legends

All the way to Aloha Stadium on the team bus, Hilary speed-read the sports section of the newspaper she had found in Junior Seau's room. Thank goodness there were a lot of pictures of the Pro Bowl players. These people were Seau's friends and colleagues. It might be nice if she recognized them.

A funny thought cut through her nervousness. There would be no problem if Nick were here. He knew everything there was to know about these athletes—birthdays, shoe sizes, old high schools, even their favorite breakfast cereals. Nick and his Get-a-Life Club buddies would probably *love* being turned into Junior Seau. They wouldn't have the sense to be as terrified as she was!

Hilary looked around the bus. Actually, you didn't have to be a huge football fan to recognize a lot of these men. They were stars of TV commercials; they were interviewed everywhere; they were spokesmen for the United Way and other major charities. Names like

Elway, Dan Marino, Drew Bledsoe, and Bruce Smith were household words. And over on the NFC bus were stars like Barry Sanders, Troy Aikman, Emmitt Smith, and Jerry Rice.

But I'm just as famous as any of these legends, she thought in amazement. *I mean, Junior Seau is.*

When the bus arrived at the stadium, she attracted as many reporters and autograph seekers as any of the all-time football greats.

For Hilary, it was an eye-opener. She knew there were defensive stars, too. But waiting for some guy to run up to you so you could knock him down didn't seem all that important—or even very hard.

A microphone appeared in front of her. She stared at the interviewer. *Why do I know this guy?*

All at once, she remembered. It was Dan Dierdorf, the famous commentator from *Monday Night Football*. She grinned. The Get-a-Life Club would have a heart attack!

In the Rifkins' basement, Nick stuffed an enormous wad of pizza into his mouth. "Look," he mumbled around all that cheese. "It's Junior Seau!"

He, Coleman, and Elliot crowded up close to the screen to watch the interview.

"Any predictions for the game, Junior?" asked Dan Dierdorf.

"Oh, uh, I'm pretty sure the NFL is going to win," number fifty-five told them.

"The NFL?" Dierdorf repeated, puzzled. "You mean the NFC?"

"Yeah, right," the linebacker agreed. "No, wait a minute! I play for the AFC, right?"

"What a kidder," laughed the commentator. "Well anyway, you've got to agree that Hawaii's a pretty nice place to be on the first of February."

The Monday Night Football Club watched their hero register deep shock. "February first? I'm missing my birthday!"

"Hey, no fooling," piped up Coleman. "Junior Seau has the same birthday as Hilary, Hilary, Heavy Artillery."

"No, he doesn't," Nick said, frowning. "Junior Seau was born on January 19, 1969, in Oceanside, California."

"He was joking," scoffed Elliot. "Look, even Dan Dierdorf's laughing."

"Not only is Junior Seau awesome," added Coleman, "but he's got a great sense of humor, too."

Nick pulled the Eskimos sweater down over his head. He unrolled his sleeping bag and crawled inside. "Turn down the volume. I want to fall asleep fast."

Elliot grinned. "You're so lucky. I wonder who you're going to switch with."

"What does it matter?" asked Coleman. "It's the Pro Bowl. It's all stars out there. I just wish there was some way we could recognize which one is you."

"Tell you what," said Nick. "When I know I'm on TV, I'll wave."

* * *

I've got to hand it to the NFL, thought Hilary. *They sure know how to throw a party.*

Aloha Stadium vibrated with the excitement of fifty thousand screaming fans. Hilary was used to girls' volleyball games in the gym of Middletown Junior High. This crowd seemed like half the population of the world by comparison.

A battalion of TV cameras pointed at the field from all angles and directions. Brass bands, hula dancers, fireworks, cheerleaders—no wonder the Monday Night Football Club was entranced by this sport. It was pure spectacle.

Hilary would have enjoyed it more if she wasn't so stiff with fright. Yes, she looked like Junior Seau; she even talked like Junior Seau. But when the game started, people were going to expect her to *play* like Junior Seau.

And I don't even know where to stand.

"Okay, defense," called Coach Bill Cowher after the kickoff. "You're on."

Hilary trotted out with the other defenders. She was dreading the words she knew might be coming: "Hey, stupid, you're facing the wrong way."

But something strange happened. When she had reached the right place on the field, Seau's legs stopped jogging. This body seemed to know its spot as clearly as if it was marked with an *X* on the grass.

She felt herself crouch into a stance not too different from a karate position. Her cleats dug into the turf, ready to spring her into action.

"Hut!"

Hilary was amazed at how twenty-two big bodies exploded into movement. The collision of linemen made the ground shake. It was total chaos. Everybody seemed to be going in a different direction. And then the bone-crushing blocks split the defense, and the runner appeared.

Hilary gawked. It was none other than the great Barry Sanders. Her heart jumped up into her throat.

She remembered her own words: *"The ballcarrier comes to you, and you tackle him. Big deal."* She could do this. It wasn't rocket science.

And sure enough, Barry Sanders came to her. With a step to the left, and a deke to the right, the NFL's top rusher shot right past her.

Hilary stood there, frozen with shock. Sanders's gain was twenty-two yards. First down, NFC.

"Hey, Junior," Cowher called from the sidelines. "If you wanted to watch, we would have bought you a ticket!"

Okay, thought Hilary. *No more Junior Nice Guy.*

"Hut, hut!"

On the second play, she burst right up into the action. The instant Barry Sanders appeared, she clamped Junior Seau's powerful arms around him. She was about to wrestle him to the ground when she realized he didn't have the ball.

I've been duped!

Quarterback Troy Aikman reared back and fired a

long pass to a streaking Jerry Rice. When the dust cleared, it was first and goal for the NFC. The ball was on the three yard line.

"This is *hard*!" Hilary blurted in frustration.

Bruce Smith of the Buffalo Bills looked at her with a crooked grin. "When was it ever easy?"

Hilary got into position once more. This time she was standing right on the goal line. You didn't have to be the Monday Night Football Club to figure out that the situation was grave.

Okay, she thought. *Maybe I was wrong. Maybe it's not so easy to play defense.*

But there was no one she could ask for advice—not without revealing that she *wasn't* Junior Seau.

Wait a minute! There is one person who can help— Junior Seau himself!

Some of Seau's instincts were still with his body. Otherwise, Hilary wouldn't even know where to line up. Maybe those same instincts could teach her how to play this game!

She went into position, fixed her eyes on the quarterback, and emptied her mind of all Hilary thoughts.

Let Junior Seau's talent take over.

"Hut!"

And everything was different. For starters, even when she wasn't moving, she was moving—bouncing lightly on her feet, ready to strike. Second, she knew where the ball was before she could see it. Hilary couldn't explain it—it was linebacker radar. And it worked.

The ballcarrier was none other than Emmitt Smith. When Hilary exploded forward to meet him, she felt like she was being fired out of a cannon. She squared her shoulders and plowed two hundred and fifty pounds of Junior Seau into the Dallas runner. One arm dragged Smith down, the other went for the ball.

Hilary pounded and swiped. And when she felt pigskin against her hand, she yanked with all Junior Seau's might.

"Fumble!" Hilary shrieked.

Seau's eagle-eyes locked onto the ball as it bounced and wobbled through a sea of scrambling feet. With a cry of determination, Hilary flung herself into a pile of players. In the pushing and shoving that followed, it was the strong hands of Junior Seau that came up with the fumble.

Hilary leaped to her feet, the ball held high. Fifty thousand fans roared their approval.

She was thinking of the Get-a-Life Club—three maniacs with the NFL logo stamped on their brains. Finally she could see what all the fuss was about.

The Pizza-Box Wall

Nick Lighter snored softly in his sleeping bag. He was dead to the world. One arm was flung up over his head, revealing the tattered brown sleeve of the Eskimos jersey.

Two giant pizza boxes were set up like a privacy fence. They separated the sleeping Nick from Coleman, Elliot, and the television set. The two knelt in front of the screen, drinking in every detail of the most exciting Pro Bowl in years. Both defensive squads were playing hard-tackling, teeth-rattling, all-out football. Going into the second quarter, the score was knotted at 7–7.

Coleman's face was screwed up in concentration. "I don't see anybody waving. Do you think we could have missed it?"

"Are you kidding?" Elliot replied. "I don't even *blink* when I'm watching football. If Nick waved, we would have noticed."

"I don't know," Coleman mused, worried. "We didn't

see the glowing football either, and that always happens when somebody switches."

"Maybe the pizza boxes were in the way," Elliot suggested. "But there are no pizza boxes in front of the TV. I'm watching. Nobody waved."

"I guess he forgot," Coleman concluded. "You remember what it's like to play in an NFL game. Everything happens so fast, huge guys are flying all over the place—if you take time to wave, someone like Junior Seau could knock your head off!"

There were heavy footsteps on the basement stairs. Mr. Rifkin peered over the banister. "Why are you sitting so close to the TV? Are you hoping one of the players will see you and wave?"

"Dad—shhhh!" Elliot put a finger to his lips. "You'll disturb Nick."

Mr. Rifkin squinted at Nick, half buried in his bedroll. "Why did he bother to come here for the game if he's only going to sleep through it?"

Coleman and Elliot exchanged a nervous glance. There was no answer to that question—at least not one you could give Mr. Rifkin.

"He's really stressed out," Coleman managed finally. "Fifth grade is a pressure cooker. It's no party like fourth grade—" Elliot's hand over his mouth stopped his babble.

"Well, get those pizza boxes into the garbage," Mr. Rifkin ordered. "This is our home, not the town dump." He stomped back up the stairs.

Coleman let out a long sigh of relief. "I was afraid he'd wake up Nick!"

"Wake up *Nick*?" Elliot repeated in a hoarse whisper. "Think, Coleman. He switched already. That's not Nick anymore. It's somebody from the Pro Bowl!"

"I forgot!" Coleman croaked. He stared intently at Nick's sleeping form. "Who do you think he is? I hope he's friendly."

"*I* hope he doesn't wake up," Elliot amended. "I don't want to have to explain this to *anybody*!"

The cheering of the Pro Bowl crowd filled the room even though the TV volume was down low. On the screen, Junior Seau steamrolled straight over his blocker and knocked NFC quarterback Steve Young flying.

"Another sack for Junior Seau!" crowed play-by-play announcer Al Michaels.

"The Pro Bowl doesn't count in the standings, but I guess nobody told Junior," chuckled Dan Dierdorf. "He's showing the excitement and intensity of a rookie in his first NFL game!"

"Did you hear that?" whispered Elliot. "Do you think Nick could be Junior Seau? I mean, Seau's not a rookie, but Nick sort of is."

"Wouldn't that be fantastic!" exclaimed Coleman. "The great Junior Seau! Imagine what it must feel like to be so *big*!" He threw his arms wide, knocking over the pizza-box wall. A corner of one of the boxes caught their sleeping friend right in the middle of the forehead.

"Ow!" Nick looked up, startled.

Coleman and Elliot each took a step back.

"Uh—uh—sorry, sir—," Coleman stammered.

Nick looked at him as though he had a cabbage for a head. "Who are you calling sir?"

"Nick?" Elliot asked in a timid voice.

"Well, of course it's me," Nick growled. "How am I supposed to switch into the Pro Bowl if you won't let me sleep?"

"But you've been asleep for forty-five minutes!" Coleman told him. "It's the second quarter already."

Nick sat up in dismay. "Something's wrong! The sweater didn't do anything!"

"Don't freak out," Elliot soothed. "Maybe you weren't really asleep. Maybe you were just dozing."

"But what if I was sleeping just fine?" Nick quavered. "What if Hilary did something to bust the shirt?"

"At least try again before we panic," Elliot advised.

"Yeah, okay."

Nick wasn't a hundred percent convinced. But anything was better than admitting that the North Brainerd Eskimos jersey could no longer perform its magic. He set up the pizza boxes and lay back down. "You know, if this doesn't work, I'll miss the whole Pro Bowl."

"It'll work," promised Elliot. "Think positive."

"We'll watch for the little football," added Coleman. "I swear I won't take my eyes off you."

But a roar from the TV dragged Coleman and Elliot back to the Pro Bowl. They watched entranced as Steve

Young fired a sixty-yard touchdown pass into the sure hands of Detroit's Herman Moore.

The extra point gave the NFC a 14–7 lead.

After several instant replays and a lot of Monday Night Football Club high fives, Coleman and Elliot turned back to Nick to watch for the glowing football.

But their friend was already fast asleep and snoring.

Linebackers Don't Take Bubble Baths

Crunch! Pow! Smash! Wham!

Those were the sounds of a typical day at the office for Junior Seau.

Hilary was a good athlete, strong and well coordinated. But never in her wildest dreams had she imagined the skill and strength of a superstar linebacker.

His sharp eyes read the offense; his quick mind made decisions in a split second; his powerful legs catapulted him into sudden action; his huge arms clamped onto their target like the jaws of a meat-eating dinosaur; and when he hit, it was instant train wreck.

Second down and six. Hilary concentrated on the NFC offensive line.

"Hut, hut, hut!"

She watched with Junior Seau's eyes as the tackles dropped back with their quarterback.

It's a pass play, she thought.

For a split second, she considered a bull run at Steve

Young. Then she saw Young's eyes flicker for just an instant to a spot between the hash marks.

Her instincts—*Junior Seau's instincts*—told her that was where the ball would be going. Sure enough, Jerry Rice was running a crossing pattern a dozen yards downfield.

Seau's body was off and moving even before the plan was clear in Hilary's mind. She leaped—not *at* Rice, but in front of him. When the bullet pass arrived, it landed with a smack in her hands. She hit the turf running.

Look at me go! Hilary thought in amazement. *I'm a charging rhino!*

She stiff-armed one tackler, then bumped another one and knocked him flat. All at once, she felt her stride open up as she flew down the sidelines. The hash marks went by quicker and quicker.

I can't believe it! she marveled. *I'm built like a tank, but I sprint like an Olympic track star!*

Hilary Lighter blasted across the goal line. Her scream of triumph was instantly swallowed up by the cheers from fifty thousand throats.

"Happy birthday, Hilary!" she howled. This was a better present than anything she could have imagined. She spiked the ball so hard that it took a divot out of the end zone of Aloha Stadium.

Halftime was relaxed and loose in the AFC locker room. The players were still celebrating Junior Seau's touchdown, which had tied the score at fourteen. Everyone felt that the AFC now had the momentum to win the game in the second half.

The greatest stars of the NFL were from many different teams. The Pro Bowl was a rare chance to get together, so the locker room was chatty.

"We were at home against the Packers," Drew Bledsoe was saying, "and my whole family flew in for the game. It was the first time my grandmother had ever watched me as a pro. On the very first snap, I got tackled into the biggest mud puddle you've ever seen. When it was over, I took everybody out to dinner. Grandma said, 'Too bad you didn't get to play, dear.' I was so filthy that my own grandmother didn't recognize me!"

Loud guffaws greeted this story.

"How about you, Junior?" prompted Bruce Smith. "What's the weirdest thing that happened to you this season?"

Uh-oh. Hilary thought fast. "Well, uh, we were playing Toledo —"

"Wait a minute," Bledsoe interrupted. "Toledo doesn't have a football team."

Hilary panicked. "Well, um, I told you it was weird."

The group of all-stars roared with laughter.

"Now that you mention weird," put in John Elway, "I had an experience this season that I still can't explain. I missed a whole *Monday Night Football* game. I mean, I was *there*. Everybody says I played great. But I don't remember any of it."

"You just blanked out the whole time?" asked Hilary.

To her, nothing was more memorable than the action on the field. She would never forget a minute of it.

Elway looked bewildered. "Not exactly blanked out. But the stuff I do remember makes no sense. I think I was lying in a sleeping bag. There were kids there, watching the game I was supposed to be in. But the thing I remember best is that I was wearing this really itchy shirt."

Hilary sat forward so suddenly that she almost fell off the bench. "An itchy shirt? Was it brown, maybe? With the number thirteen?"

Elway shrugged. "I don't know. I'm pretty sure I was asleep. But man, was it itchy! Just talking about it makes my skin crawl!" He stared at her. "Don't tell me it happened to you, too!"

"Oh, uh—not really," stammered Hilary. But an itchy shirt? A sleeping bag? Kids watching *Monday Night Football*? That sounded like the Get-a-Life Club!

The players continued to discuss weird game experiences, but they had lost Hilary. Her mind was a whirlwind of crazy thoughts. How could a celebrity like John Elway get mixed up in one of the Monday Night Football Club's weekly pajama parties? It was impossible.

Yes, but look at *her* day so far. She had started off in karate class and ended up in the body of an all-pro linebacker, seven thousand miles from home. That was just as impossible. Maybe more.

But both "impossibles" had one thing in common— an itchy shirt.

And suddenly, it all came clear, like driving out of a dark tunnel into bright sunshine.

It was the sweater! Grandpa's ugly, scratchy, miserable old football jersey had some kind of magic! Whoever wore it would trade places with a football star! One of those Get-a-Life Clubbers must have switched himself with John Elway. That's how Elway had ended up in the middle of Monday Night Club.

It all made sense! No wonder Grandpa had given the shirt to his lawyers to lock in a vault. That moth-eaten old rag had supernatural powers! There probably wasn't anything like it in the whole world!

She frowned, suddenly furious. How could those little squirts keep something like this from her? Just as suddenly, she grinned. When they found out she had hijacked their big secret and was now Junior Seau—

Wait a minute! If she was *here* playing in the Pro Bowl, where did that leave the real Junior Seau?

Sitting on a chair decked with ribbons and paper flowers, Junior Seau was opening presents.

"Oh, wow, bubble bath. Thanks a lot."

Well, he was still trapped in this life—still Hilary. But at least none of these friends suspected that he was an impostor.

A girl named Barbara pointed to the delicate bottle of dark red liquid. "See? It's Cinnamon Valentine, the newest fragrance from Bubble Bunnies."

"That's great," said Seau. He hoped he sounded sincere. These girls seemed so keen on Hilary's having a good time at her birthday party. He didn't have the heart to tell them that most linebackers didn't take scented bubble baths.

Katrina placed another beribboned parcel in front of him. "Come on, Hilary. Let's finish opening these. The guys will be here soon. They're watching some dumb football game."

Seau's heart leaped. "The Pro Bowl?"

"Whatever. Anyway, they're coming at nine. And they're bringing a really special surprise for the birthday girl."

Junior Seau dropped the bubble bath in the pocket of his shirt—or was it a blouse? He groaned inwardly. He'd already had enough surprises for one day.

Crunch Time

The NFC came out flying in the second half. Quarterback Brett Favre of the Green Bay Packers marched his team quickly down the field. That led to a touchdown run by Barry Sanders, and a 21–14 lead.

Suddenly, Hilary found herself in the role of cheerleader. She put Junior Seau's considerable bulk into clapping, towel waving, and shouting encouragement to her offense. But the NFC defense was a toughness Who's Who. It was anchored by Reggie White, Kevin Greene, and Simeon Rice. The NFC held firm, forcing the AFC to settle for a field goal.

"Twenty-one to seventeen," muttered Coach Cowher. "Not good enough."

All through the third quarter and into the fourth, football's very best did battle. The finest defensive backs jumped to steal passes from the top receivers. The strongest linemen fought off the deadliest blitzers. The greatest tacklers hurled themselves at the most sure-footed runners. Both sides staged impressive drives. But neither team scored.

It took the leading passer in NFL history to break the deadlock. As the setting sun dipped below the grandstand of Aloha Stadium, Dan Marino dropped back into the pocket. With a lightning release, he sizzled a perfect spiral right through a crowd of players into the chest of Terry Glenn in the end zone. AFC 24, NFC 21.

The clatter of helmet bonks on the AFC sidelines drowned out the roar of the crowd. Hilary bonked right along with them, the harder the better. She smashed Chris Spielman so hard that she knocked his face mask loose.

"Oops, sorry," she said sheepishly. "I guess I don't know my own strength."

Well, Junior Seau's strength.

The AFC kickoff coverage team charged downfield like a herd of thundering buffalo. They smothered the return man at his own twelve-yard line. The two-minute warning sounded.

The PA system burst into life. "Flag on the play."

It was an illegal block on the runback. The penalty moved the ball half the distance to the goal line.

Hilary's mind raced as she got into position. *The NFC is jammed up at their own six. This is the perfect time for a blitz!*

Bruce Smith must have been thinking the same thing. At the snap he exploded from his stance, flushing

Brett Favre out of the pocket. Favre tucked away the ball and scrambled from danger, right at —

Me! thought Hilary. She sprang ahead only to find not one, but *two* big linemen in her path.

No fair! she wanted to howl. *Just because I'm having a great game, they're throwing a whole extra guy at me!*

Then she remembered: Hilary Lighter had never faced a double-team before. But Junior Seau had. Sure enough, the great linebacker's reflexes clicked on, taking her along for the ride.

She rammed her shoulder pad into the first blocker and bulled forward. This drove the lineman back into his teammate, knocking them both off balance. Then she spun like a figure skater and launched herself at the quarterback. But Favre leaped, and Hilary landed hard on the grass in the end zone beneath him.

With a cry of determination, Hilary reached up blindly. She grabbed a leg and yanked with all Junior Seau's might. Favre came crashing to the turf beside her.

In the Rifkin basement, Coleman and Elliot rocketed to their feet for a flying double high five.

"What a sack!" they chorused.

"What a *safety!*" Elliot amended. "Junior sacked him in the end zone! That's two more points for the AFC."

"They're ahead by five! Now the NFC can't tie it up with a field goal!" raved Coleman. "They need a touchdown to win the game! Junior's awesome! He's out of control—"

He was interrupted by a pizza box bouncing off his head. Coleman and Elliot wheeled. Nick was on his feet, staring red-faced at them.

"*You're* the ones who are out of control!" he raged. "Our shirt might be busted, and I can't even test it because you maniacs won't let me sleep!"

Coleman was horrified. "You mean you *still* haven't switched?"

"Maybe you switched, and now you're back," added Elliot.

Nick shook his head miserably. "Not unless I traded places with someone who's been unconscious for the last hour. Face it—the sweater is no good."

"Sorry," mumbled Elliot. "We didn't mean to wake you. It's just that Junior Seau just made a move—I can't even describe it. Here, watch the replay."

Nick was so down that he could barely bring himself to pay attention. There was a hollow ache in the pit of his stomach—the same kind of pain that spicy food gave Coleman. Only Coleman's heartburn always went away. The kid with the same initials as the NFL knew that a lot of Pro Bowls would have to go by before he would ever get used to life without the magic sweater.

On TV, the safety was replayed in slow-motion. The triumphant number fifty-five leaped up in the air, executing a double karate kick.

Nick gawked. "Did you see that?"

"Amazing," agreed Elliot. "But I feel terrible about—"

"Not the sack!" Nick cut him off. "The kick! That's my sister's new karate thing! She does it all the time!"

Coleman was confused. "But why would Junior Seau be doing Hilary's martial arts move?"

Nick snapped his fingers. "The shirt isn't busted."

"Then why won't it work?" challenged Elliot.

"Because it's already working," Nick supplied. "For Hilary."

"For *Hilary*?" Coleman repeated. "She doesn't even know what the sweater can do."

"It must have happened by accident," Nick explained. "She got cold, put it on, fell asleep—and now she's Junior Seau!"

The Monday Night Football Club stared at the TV. Somewhere inside that six-foot-three, two-hundred-fifty-pound frame was Nick's eighth-grade sister.

"It's hard to imagine," said Coleman.

"You know what's even harder to imagine?" put in Elliot. "The real Junior Seau is the guest of honor at Hilary's birthday party. He's going to love Seth Kroppman jumping out of a cake!"

"Hilary's lucky," Coleman said wistfully. "She's right there for one of the greatest Pro Bowls of all time."

"Maybe she's not so lucky," frowned Elliot. "Think about it: she changed by accident. That means she doesn't know how to change back!"

The three exchanged worried looks. To reverse the effect of the Eskimos sweater, both "switchees" had to get clobbered at the same instant. That would be no problem for Hilary. As Junior Seau in the Pro Bowl, she was giving and taking bruising hits every second. But the real Junior Seau was a fourteen-year-old girl at a birthday party. "She" wasn't even wearing the shirt anymore.

"We've got to crash that party," Nick concluded.

"Are you crazy?" Coleman exploded. "We promised we'd stay away. If we set foot in your house, the whole eighth grade is going to kill us."

"This is my sister we're talking about," Nick said stoutly. "Yeah, sure, she's a big pain. But I don't want to lose her *forever*!"

"Plus it wouldn't exactly be fair to Junior Seau, either," Elliot added. "How'd you like to be demoted from the San Diego Chargers to Middletown Junior High?"

"Well, couldn't we at least wait until after the party?" wheedled Coleman. "I don't want to face all those eighth graders. They're twice our size! Half of them have mustaches—and those are just the *girls*—"

Nick shook his head. "We need to do it *now*, during the Pro Bowl. The NFC has time for one more drive. We have that long to sneak into the party, get the shirt on Hilary, and zap her while Junior Seau's still taking hits!"

"You mean zap *Junior* while *Hilary's* taking hits," Elliot corrected. "They're switched, remember?"

"Right," Nick nodded. "Simple?"

"Simple as brain surgery with a hammer and chisel," Elliot agreed with a groan.

"Here's another problem," challenged Coleman.

"What do we tell Elliot's parents? What's our excuse for running out on the Pro Bowl at nine o'clock at night?"

In answer, Elliot ran to his father's basement workshop and came back with a stepladder. He set it down against the wall, climbed the four steps, and pushed open the narrow basement window. "They'll never know we've been gone," he whispered down.

"No coats?" croaked Coleman. "What about my scratchy throat?"

"Tell your scratchy throat not to be such a wimp," Nick ordered. "We're only going a couple of blocks."

The Monday Night Football Club scrambled up the ladder and out the window. Hugging their shoulders and shivering, they disappeared into the night.

A Piece of Cake

Hilary and the AFC defense braced for the most furious attack of the Pro Bowl.

First down: no gain. Second down: incomplete pass. Third down: sack! Loss of six yards.

And then it was fourth down. She looked at the scoreboard.

Fifteen seconds to victory!

The message pounded with every beat of Junior Seau's heart.

"Hut, hut!" barked Brett Favre.

Hilary blitzed, spinning off her blocker. But Favre had been expecting it. He rolled out of the pocket, rearing back to throw.

She leaped high in the air, raising her hands to knock down the pass. Favre's arm came forward, and —

Oh no! Hilary thought in midair. *He didn't release the ball! He just double-pumped to fake me out!*

Crash! She hit the turf. She tried desperately to

scramble back up, but it was too late. Favre danced around her and launched a long bomb.

For a moment, there was dead silence in Aloha Stadium. Fifty thousand pairs of eyes followed the pass. It sailed in a graceful arc high above the field. Then—a deafening roar. The ball dropped into the outstretched hands of Jerry Rice.

"Hit him!" screamed Hilary in Junior Seau's deep voice.

But tackling Jerry Rice in the open field was no easy task. Cornerbacks and safeties dove into number eighty's path. Rice cut, hurdled, and stiff-armed around, over, and through them. When Pittsburgh's Carnell Lake finally made the tackle, the ball was spotted on the one-and-a-half yard line.

The NFC called its final time-out. Four seconds remained on the clock.

"It's all my fault," moaned Hilary in the huddle. "I can't believe I fell for that little fake! I should've sacked him. I should've deflected the pass! I should've —"

"Take it easy, Junior," interrupted Bruce Smith.

"Easy?" she echoed, aghast. "We're a yard and a half away from *losing*! For guys like Barry Sanders and Emmitt Smith, that might as well be a millionth of an inch!"

"What's the big deal?" asked one of the linemen. "The Pro Bowl doesn't count as an *official* game."

"You can't think about it that way!" Hilary raged.

"Well, how *should* we think about it?" the man asked.

"The way *I* do!" she bawled. "Like it's a miracle! Like you're here by some weird mistake, and this is the last down of NFL football you're ever going to play, and the next time you put on a sports uniform it's going to say Middletown Junior High Girls' Volleyball!"

The AFC defenders looked at her in confusion.

"Girls' volleyball?" Lake repeated.

"I think I know what Junior's trying to say," Bruce Smith began slowly. "How many people get to make their living playing a game they love? Man, we're the luckiest guys on earth—and the Pro Bowl is our chance to say thank you to our teams and our fans."

"When you put it that way," Lake nodded, "I agree with Junior. This next snap is as big as any Super Bowl."

"Thanks, Junior," added the lineman. "Thanks for reminding me what's *really* important."

"AFC!" cried Hilary, holding Junior Seau's meaty fist above their heads. It was joined by ten others, and soon the chant came from the entire defensive team.

"AFC! . . . AFC! . . ."

The three Monday Night Football Club members peered around the Lighters' garage at the front door. Katrina was ushering at least ten eighth-grade boys into the house.

"No way we can sneak in there," Elliot whispered.

"Whatever we do, let's do it fast," hissed Coleman. "I'm freezing!"

"I'm totally fine," Nick observed in surprise. "My grandpa's sweater is warmer than whale blubber."

"Yeah, well, right now I'd settle for a little whale blubber," shivered Elliot. "Do you think we could slip into the living room through the French doors?"

The Monday Night Football Club raced around the side of garage. Suddenly, Nick put on the brakes, and Coleman and Elliot rammed him from behind.

There, outside the glass doors, sat the big wooden cake. It was purple with pink trim—the "icing" had been painted a color so bright that it glowed like a neon sign.

The three ducked into the bushes.

"It's awesome," whispered Elliot. "Just like a real cake, only bigger."

"I'm getting hungry just looking at it," added Coleman. "I told you we should have ordered double pepperoni on the pizzas."

The lid was open like the hatch of a submarine, and Seth Kroppman's upper body stuck out. He glared at the two eighth-graders with him.

"But yesterday you lifted me, no problem," Seth was saying.

"We lifted *you*, not the cake," his friend pointed out. "All that wood makes extra weight, you know."

"Come on," prompted Seth. "Put some muscle into it!"

"Listen, bro," the other lifter complained. "It's bad enough we have to miss the end of the Pro Bowl to help you get back your girlfriend. We're not going to break our necks doing it."

"Okay, okay, go get another guy," Seth told them. "But be quiet about it! We don't want to spoil the surprise for Hilary."

The lifters disappeared inside the French doors. Nick put his arms around the shaking shoulders of his fellow Monday Night Football Club members. "I have a plan."

"Are you nuts?" Elliot rasped. "There are thirty of them and only three of us! How can we get inside without being seen?"

Nick smiled. "It's a piece of cake."

It was hard to pace in a wooden cake four feet wide, but Seth was managing. He walked in small, nervous circles. This idea was the perfect chance to make up with Hilary. He hoped his friends wouldn't say anything stupid and ruin it.

Pow!

The snowball came out of nowhere and smacked him right in the head.

"What the—," he sputtered. "Who did that?"

Another heavy wet bomb thumped into his chin, spraying slush all over his face. Now he could hear voices. What were they saying?

"Take that, Kroppman, you loser!"

"This next one's going straight down your throat!"

Seth cleared the snow from his eyes and stared in shock. He was under attack from a couple of *fifth-graders*! Sidekicks of Hilary's little brother! They were running around like lunatics with no coats or gloves!

"Have you guys lost your minds?" Seth cried in disbelief.

In answer, a barrage of snowballs smacked into his head and shoulders.

"Come and get us, Kroppman, you big wimp!" taunted Elliot. "What are you—chicken?"

Coleman made loud clucking sounds, flapping his arms like wings.

"That does it!" roared Seth. In a rage, he leaped out of the cake and sprinted across the lawn.

Coleman and Elliot turned tail and ran, their sneakers slipping and sliding in the ice and snow. The much bigger Seth thundered after them, howling with fury.

When the coast was clear, Nick picked himself up out of the bushes and scampered over to the cake. He climbed inside and pulled the lid shut above him. Squatting, he struggled out of the Eskimos sweater.

There were voices outside, followed by a knock on the lid of the cake. "Hey, Seth." It was one of the lifters from before. "You ready?"

"Mm, hmm," murmured Nick. He hoped he sounded like Seth—or at least *not* like Nick Lighter.

He felt the floor of the wooden cake lift up off the patio.

"Yo, bro," came the voice again, "it feels like you've lost some weight."

Nick held his breath. Would he be found out?

A laugh. "Get real, Einstein. There's three of us now. Of course he seems lighter."

Inside the house, Katrina was steering Junior Seau toward his surprise. Her free hand covered his eyes. "This is it, Hilary!" she exclaimed like a circus ringmaster. She whipped her palm away. *"Ta-da!"*

Junior Seau gawked at the giant purple-and-pink cake.

Hidden in its belly, Nick reached up to fling open the lid.

Half Running, Half *Flying*

The crowd noise in Aloha Stadium was as loud as in any closed dome. You didn't just *hear* sound like that; it got in through your ears and filled your whole body. Hilary was as pumped as the Goodyear Blimp overhead.

How many times did I make fun of Nick for staying up to watch the last four seconds of a Monday Night Football *game?* she wondered. Now she knew that four seconds might as well be forever when the score was 26–21.

Just a few hours ago, she had been convinced that defense wasn't very important in a football game. Yet there on the sidelines stood John Elway and Dan Marino. Two of the greatest of all time—but they could do nothing but watch and pray. This battle rested in the hands of the foot soldiers. The Pro Bowl was theirs to win!

Or lose, if we allow a touchdown.

She gritted Junior Seau's teeth. It couldn't happen! It *wouldn't* happen! Not if Hilary Lighter had anything to say about it!

With a little help from Junior Seau!

"Hut!"

This was it! Linemen connected. Blocks were thrown, players hit the turf.

Here comes Barry Sanders! Here comes Emmitt Smith!

Which star had the ball? Hilary looked around desperately.

I've got to do something! I can't just stand here while we lose the game!

But Seau's body refused to react. All at once, Hilary realized why. Her linebacker instincts were making her wait!

It's going to be a pass!

Then she saw the receiver—Herman Moore, all alone, right in front of the goal line.

Favre threw, and Hilary erupted, half running, half *flying*. She clamped her thick arms around Moore just as the ball whapped into his hands. Three NFC players hurled themselves at their teammate to knock him forward into the end zone.

The terrible moment seemed to freeze time in Hilary's mind. She couldn't stop the push of three huge guys! It would take an earthquake! A bulldozer! Either that or . . . or . . .

Junior Seau!

With a cry of *"AFC!!"* she hurled Moore away from the end zone with an explosion of strength that would have toppled the pyramids. The receiver flew back, right into his three teammates. All four of them went down, and so did Hilary. Big bodies shook the turf like concussion bombs. And the last thing she saw was that one of the bombs was going to land right on top of her.

We won! she thought ecstatically. And then everything went dark.

"Happy Birthday!" Nick threw open the lid of the cake and leaped up.

"Nick?!" shrieked Katrina.

He brought the Eskimos sweater down over the figure of Hilary that he knew to be Junior Seau. But her head caught in one of the sleeves. The shirt wouldn't go on all the way.

"Get out of that cake, Nick!" wailed Katrina.

Angry eighth-grade arms reached for him. Desperately, Nick climbed out of the cake and jumped at Seau, trying to yank down the jersey. Instead, the blinded linebacker caught him in midair. With Nick in his arms and the wool in his face, Seau staggered backwards into the hall. His sneaker slipped in a puddle of spilled soda, and his legs flew out from under him. Wham! He landed flat on his back, with Nick tumbling on top of him.

The tiny glowing football began its dance over the brown fabric. Hands shaking, Nick straightened the sweater and pulled down the neck, revealing his sister's head.

"Hilary, is that you?" he asked urgently.

There was the sound of a key in the lock. The door

opened, and Mr. and Mrs. Lighter stepped into the house. The sight that met their eyes appalled them: Nick, with his dazed sister in a wrestling hold, shaking her by the collar.

"All right, that does it!" roared Mr. Lighter. "I warned you two what would happen if we caught you fighting again!"

His wife's attention was on something else. "What is this terrible mess? Where is that music coming from?" Her high heels crunched in the chip crumbs as she marched forward into the living room. She yanked the plug from the wall, and the stereo fell silent.

"Awwwwwww."

Thirty-two eighth-grade complaints were swallowed in an instant. Mrs. Lighter's face was a thundercloud Nick knew too well. When Dad lost his temper, he got loud. But Mom was just the opposite. The angrier she got, the quieter she became. It was ten times worse than yelling.

She announced, "This party is over."

Her voice was barely a whisper.

13

Call an Ambulance

"What a spectacular finish!" Al Michaels raved in the broadcast booth of Aloha Stadium. "Junior Seau made that stop *one inch* from the goal line! The AFC wins!"

The victorious players ran out onto the field. There were backslaps and helmet bonks, but the champions were saving the real congratulations for the man of the hour.

They joined the officials, who were helping to disentangle the mountain of all-stars from the pile. One by one, the Pro Bowlers got up, shaking off the big collision. All except . . .

"Someone's hurt," announced Frank Gifford.

"It's Junior Seau," added Dan Dierdorf in concern.

The players and coaches of both sides rushed to the aid of the fallen hero. The team doctor rolled Seau over onto his back. A gasp of shock went up in Aloha Stadium.

The front of Seau's jersey was soaked dark red. The

stain covered the number fifty-five on his chest and trickled down his white pants.

"He's losing blood!" cried the doctor. "Call an ambulance!"

The doctor carefully removed Seau's helmet. He waved a small tube of smelling salts to wake the injured man up.

"Junior?"

Seau blinked once. Everything was just a blur. "Where's the kid who jumped out of the cake?"

"Oh, man," breathed John Elway. "He's really messed up!"

"I know that voice!" Suddenly, the big linebacker leaped to his feet. He enfolded the Broncos quarterback in a bear hug, smearing red on Elway's uniform. "John, you'll never know how happy I am to see you! Has the game started yet?"

"Started? It's over!" The doctor grabbed him by the shoulders and tried to ease him back down to the field. Seau wouldn't budge.

"Listen to the doctor," Elway pleaded. "You got creamed on the last play. You're bleeding really bad."

The linebacker stared at him. "No, I'm not!"

"Look!" Elway pulled up the bottom of Seau's jersey, showing him the deep crimson stain.

Seau jumped back in shock. How could he be bleeding? He felt fine. Better even—he had his old self back. What a relief that was!

He was aware of a strange smell. A very unfootball

smell. He sniffed. A kind of soapy, flowery, cinnamon scent.

And what was that pressing against his chest? It was jagged, scratchy . . .

He reached inside his sweater. An object was caught the laces of his shoulder pads. He pulled out a flattened plastic bottle. Dark red liquid was spilling from it.

It was the bubble bath—from Hilary's party! He had put it in his pocket, and it had made the trip back to his real life in the Pro Bowl! It must have gotten crushed during the last tackle!

"That's not blood!" he exclaimed to the bewildered group around him. "It's bubble bath! Cinnamon Valentine!"

Elway goggled. "What?"

Seau held up the smashed gift. "It's the newest fragrance from Bubble Bunnies."

The quarterback was bug-eyed. "What are you doing with bubble bath in the Pro Bowl?"

Junior Seau didn't answer. It would be impossible to explain that he had received it as a fourteenth-birthday present.

All thirty-two partygoers were officially kicked out of the Lighter house. Luckily, his mother's lecture on "treating someone else's home with respect" gave Nick a chance to hustle his dazed sister onto the couch in the TV room.

"Hilary?" He gently slapped her cheeks. "Hil?"

Her eyelids fluttered. Aloha Stadium was replaced by her own home and Nick. "Doofus, have I got a story for you!"

Nick smiled back. "I already know."

Mr. Lighter stuck his head into the room. "Look at you two, suddenly all buddy-buddy best friends. Well, it's not going to work. We warned you about your fighting, and now you're grounded! Two weeks—is that clear?"

"But, Dad—," Hilary protested.

Nick's heart skipped a beat. Would his sister spill the beans about Grandpa's shirt? Hilary was so nuts about her friends and her social life—who knew what she'd say to get out of being grounded?

"But what?" asked Mr. Lighter.

Her face twisted. "Nothing," she said finally. "We're sorry for fighting."

"Yeah," added Nick. "Sorry, Dad."

When they were alone, Nick couldn't help hugging her.

"Why, Doofus," she laughed. "I didn't think you were the sentimental type."

"Thanks for not telling," he said with relief.

"It's funny," she reflected. "We've kept a million secrets *from* each other, but this is the first time we've ever both been in on the same one. It's almost like we're teammates or something."

"Now you sound like Junior Seau," grinned Nick.

She whistled. "What a superstar! I had the time of

my life! And believe me, I needed it. Talk about a lousy birthday! I didn't get so much as a card from my so-called friends!"

"But, Hilary—"

Nick took his sister by the hand and led her into the living room. She gawked at the wreckage of the party. Crushed chips and torn wrapping paper soaked up the puddles of spilled soda. Half-empty drinks stood on shelves, tables, and the mountain of opened presents. Much of the banner had been ripped from the wall. With so many missing letters it now proclaimed:

HILARY

EAT S FRIE D

HA IR

"It used to be a lot more, you know, flattering," Nick assured her.

"A surprise party?" she managed to say. "For me?"

Nick nodded. "But you weren't around. I'm sure Junior Seau ate your share of the ice cream."

Hilary's eyes fell on the big wooden cake. She stared at her missing baby pictures. Shamefaced, she lowered her eyes to the trampled streamers on the floor. "*That's* why you stole them? For this?"

Nick shot her a dazzling smile. "Wash the dishes for two weeks, and we'll call it even."

She shook her head in disbelief. "My own birthday party, and I missed the whole thing."

"Well," said Nick. "At least you'll get to clean it up."

All at once, there was a pounding at the glass door. Brother and sister wheeled. There, outside, stood an angry Seth Kroppman. By the scruff of the neck, he had hold of two snow creatures, white from head to toe.

Hilary scrambled to let them in. The snow creatures shook off their frosty coatings to reveal Coleman and Elliot, soaked and shivering.

"I was just about to get into the cake when these two little jerkfaces ambushed me!" Seth raged. "Oh—uh, happy birthday, Hilary." He turned burning eyes on Nick. "And *there's* the chief jerkface who put them up to it!"

He advanced menacingly on Nick, but Hilary stepped in his way.

"Nobody messes with my brother except me."

Seth's jaw dropped. "But—but he's a rat—"

"Maybe so," Hilary cut him off. "But he's *my* rat! And I've got some more news for you, Seth. I'm breaking up with you."

He staggered back. "Breaking up? We haven't even got back together yet!"

"That's better still!" roared Hilary. "It'll save me the trouble!"

"But—"

Hilary pointed out the French doors. *"Scram!"*

As Seth slunk out, the Monday Night Football Club

shared a whispered chorus of "Hilary, Hilary, Heavy Artillery."

"You've got that right," she agreed with a double karate kick. "After spending a day as Junior Seau, I'm the heaviest artillery there is!"

14

Your Loving Sister

Coleman and Elliot gazed bleakly out the front window of the Lighter house. The weather had turned suddenly warm, and the offensive line of snowmen was slowly melting away. As they watched, the carrot nose dropped off the Cool Receiver.

"Our icemen!" sniffled Coleman. His scratchy throat was quickly becoming a full-blown cold, thanks to his snow bath from Seth.

"This stinks," Elliot added. "We'll never complete the Arctic Iceman Cool Receiver Screen Pass now."

Nick's anguished voice rang out from the kitchen. "But, Dad, our icemen are turning to slush! Who ever heard of a mushy offensive line?"

"No buts, Nicky," Mr. Lighter replied. "You're *grounded*. That means you don't leave the house except for school."

"But it's only the front lawn," Nick wheedled.

"Rules are rules," his father insisted. "Look at Hilary. She isn't having any trouble taking her punishment like an adult."

Nick made a face. "That's because her hobby is blabbing on the phone to her three zillion friends. Mine is football! Trick plays! *Outside!*"

But Mr. Lighter was adamant. Nick slunk out of the kitchen with the official report: the Arctic Iceman Cool Receiver Screen Pass would have to be delayed until the next big snow.

Elliot put a sympathetic arm around his shoulders. "Take it easy. This is the roughest time of year. The Pro Bowl is so awesome, and then—boom. No football for six months."

"We can't even use the Eskimos shirt," Nick moaned. "Who wants to switch with a quarterback when he's playing golf or on vacation with his family?"

They waved to the mailman as he wheeled his cart up the walk. A handful of letters dropped through the slot in the front door.

Nick picked them up and began to flip through them. "Junk, junk, bills, Hilary, junk, junk—*whoa!!*" His face lit up like a sunrise. "It's from Junior Seau! He answered my fan letter!"

"This is just what we need to cheer us up!" raved Coleman.

"Careful not to rip it," Elliot advised as Nick opened the envelope. The founder of the Monday Night Football Club unfolded the note by the corners, as if the paper was made of the finest, most delicate lace. They stared.

> Dear Doofus,
>> Got you last!
>>> Your loving sister,
>>>> Junior Seau.

There was an agonizing silence. Then Nick threw back his head and bellowed, *"Hil-a-ry!!!"*

The Official NFL Monday Night Football Club Story of Junior Seau, San Diego Superstar

The last thing an NFL ballcarrier wants to see is Junior Seau in front of him. And if he does, Junior is the last thing he sees. One of the fiercest and hardest-working players in the NFL, Seau (pronounced *SAY-ow*) isn't going to let the ballcarrier get by him. His tackling ability and all-out hustle have made him one of the NFL's greatest defensive players.

When he was born on January 19, 1969, he was named Tiaina Seau, Jr., but he's been known as Junior since then. He was born outside of San Diego, California, but moved to the South Pacific island of Samoa, where his parents originally came from. Junior lived on Samoa until he was seven. He didn't learn to speak English until he returned to the U.S., but then he learned both English and football quickly.

As a linebacker and tight end for Oceanside High School in California, he was one of the best players in the nation. He also was a standout basketball player and was named to the state all-academic team with a 3.6 grade point average. He went to the University of Southern California, where Junior was an all-American as a junior. When he was chosen by the San Diego Chargers in the 1990 NFL draft, Seau was the fifth overall pick. He earned a Pro Bowl selection in his second season, and has been back to the annual all-star game every season since.

In 1994, Seau had a career-high 155 tackles while helping the Chargers reach Super Bowl XXIX. And in 1996, Seau had one of his best seasons yet. His seven sacks were a career high, and he tied career bests with three fumble recoveries and two interceptions, while earning his sixth Pro Bowl selection.

Junior's Honors

Six Pro Bowls / 1994 NFL Man of the Year / 1992, 1993 NFLPA Linebacker of the Year / 1992 AFC Defensive Player of the Year

Seau by the Numbers

	Tackles	Sacks	Int.	FR	TD
1996	138	7	2	3	0
Career	867	27	8	11	1

The Junior Seau Foundation

The San Diego community has given a lot to me and my family, so I try to give something back. Through the Junior Seau Foundation, we try to educate and empower young people all over our hometown. The Scholarship of Excellence helps local students attend colleges all over the nation. I'm the host of the Inner City Games, too. At this event, we encourage kids to say yes to health and fitness and no to gangs, drugs, and violence. The games also raise money to build fitness centers for kids in San Diego. On Steak and Burger Night, we raise money for the Oceanside Boys and Girls Club, where I went when I was a kid. There's more that we do in the foundation, and a lot more we can do to help young people. If you'd like to find out more about our programs, or find out how you can help, write to the Junior Seau Foundation, 2365 Northside Drive, Suite 203, San Diego, CA 92108.

Thank you!

Don't forget to tackle all of the NFL/ABC Monday Night Football books!

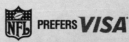

Join the hottest team around!

The Monday Night Football Club

Available Now

Monday Night Football Club #1
Quarterback Exchange:
I Was John Elway
ISBN 0-7868-1236-2

Monday Night Football Club #2
Running Back Conversion:
I Was Barry Sanders
ISBN 0-7868-1237-0

Monday Night Football Club #3
Super Bowl Switch:
I Was Dan Marino
ISBN 0-7868-1238-9

Monday Night Football Club #4
Heavy Artillery:
I Was Junior Seau
ISBN 0-7868-1259-1

Look for new books coming down the field every other month!

Monday Night Football Club #5
Ultimate Scoring Machine:
I Was Jerry Rice
ISBN 0-7868-1270-2
March 1998

Monday Night Football Club #6
NFL Magic: Bloopers, Pranks,
Upsets, and Touchdowns
ISBN 0-7868-1271-0
May 1998

Catch this!

Every book comes packed with
coupons and 800-numbers for
exclusive NFL offers on official
apparel like jerseys, hats, shirts and
shorts, or other gear plus freebies
from the League and lots of inside
stuff you can't get anywhere else.

Available at your local bookstore
$3.95 each

Get off the sidelines and onto the field with NFL.COM

NFL.COM is the official website of the National Football League and the ultimate on-line destination for football fans. From late-breaking news to comprehensive team profiles to live scores and play-by-play every game day, NFL.COM covers it all. Fans can interact with their favorite players, sound off in polls, and chat about the "big game." Plus, Play Football! covers the game for the NFL's youngest fans. Filled with fun games, stats, and trivia, the Play Football! area of NFL.COM is hot!

Check out NFL.COM for links to the Monday Night Football Club to find out which football star the guys will switch with next!

NFL Flag presented by Nike

Get into flag football competition with the NFL Flag program. Competitive leagues and instruction are divided into appropriate age groups for boys and girls age 6–14.

Leagues take place in the fall and spring in Arizona, Carolina, Chicago, Cincinnati, Cleveland, Dallas, Denver, Jacksonville, Kansas City, Miami, New England, Philadelphia, and San Diego.

For information on how to get involved, call 1-800-NFL-SNAP

Score an NFL Fan Packet today!

Get the scoop on all your favorite players with your own NFL Fan Packet, filled with the hot inside info you can't get anywhere else.

For your free NFL Fan Packet, send your name and address and favorite team name to the following address:

NFL Fan Packet
Starline Sports Marketing
1480 Terrell Rd., Marietta, GA 30067